Dedication:
For everyone who has
closed their eyes
and wished for something
seemingly outside
their power.

Foreword:

This is a selection of some of the spells I have written over the years, a collection of the ones that have grown dear to me. A lot of my personal craft focuses on feelings and my relationships with other people. Each one I've written is a little piece of my craft, and means something different to me.

Before I was a witch, when I was a child, my parents would take me to church, I had some trouble grappling with theism. At one point, I decided, the idea of god must be the way people interact with one another. When you brush hands with someone walking, stranger or not, meeting someone's eyes across the room to glance away, the communion you feel with strangers on the subway, rolling your eyes and groaning with exasperation when there's a delay. Love is in every glance, every touch, in the mere presence of other people.

I think love in all its forms and other such tender, delicate feelings are perhaps the root of magic, for me at least. Power or control may easily and just as validly be the point of witchcraft for another witch. Even before I decided to be a witch, my craft, my magic would hinge on love. The little attempts at magic I would do, wishing on stars for my cat to curl up with me, blowing dandelion seeds in the air hoping for more time with my friends, blowing out birthday candles and hoping it would draw whatever student I had a crush on that week closer.

I hope you are happy to use some of these spells, and that others of these you will never need, but should you, that they will help.

These spells, as well as witchcraft tips, guides, and some personal thoughts are also up on my blog *orriculum.tumblr.com*, as well as my other book, "Of Witchcraft and Whimsy".

Table of Contents:

ANTI-LOVE SPELLS

PLATONIC LOVE / FRIENDSHIP

FOR HELP WITH RELATIONSHIPS

FOR SOUR RELATIONSHIPS

SELF LOVE

SELF CARE - HABITS

SELF CARE - EMOTIONAL

HEALING

GENDER & ORIENTATION SPELLS

CURSES

Romantic Spells

Simple Love Attraction Spell

A spell for attracting general love and romantic opportunities to oneself. This spell does not affect a specific person, even if you have one in mind.

Gather:

- o   a pink candle
- o   rose petals
- o   pepper

Set the ingredients before you, and dress the candle wick with the pepper. Carve a heart shape onto the candle, and focus on any romantic longings you may have had.

Decorate the candle with the rose petals, offering them to your preferred deity of romantic love. Light the candle, feel it's warmth but be careful not to burn yourself. Whisper softly the incantation:

"As I watch the flame dance
I draw to me hopes of romance.
As it warms my face, I'll warm others hearts,
Who graze the feathers of cupid's dart."

Blow out the candle, thank your chosen deity for their influence.

Cosmic Love Spell

Working with the theory that there are many possible soulmates in the world, as you are an ever changing being, this is a spell designed to draw one to you. It is best performed at night, among the stars and the moon.

Gather:

- Five candles, of varying colors if you wish
- Five objects that represent a key aspect of your personality.
- A partially transparent cloth

Create a pentagram, and at each of the five points, place a candle, and a token of something that represents a key aspect of your personality.

Light a corresponding candle by each.

Mix rose petals, thyme, peach, lemongrass, and bay leaf together. Burn a pinch of the mixture in each candle.

Cover your eyes with a cloth you can only see slightly through.

Close your eyes, watch the stars in your eyes and interpret them as one would interpret tea leaves. This will be your "map" that will lead you to them.

"Sweet, My Sweet" Spell

A spell of sharing sweets to silently impart one's feelings to another

Gather:

- o sweet food such as candy or cakes
- o morning dew
- o a white candle
- o flower petals indicative of your feelings

Arrange the sweets around the candle, and the flower petals around the food in a pattern to your liking

Light the candle, and anoint the petals with dew. Gather the energies and push them into the food.

Blow out the candle, seal the charmed food with a kiss. Share the food with a willing, consenting companion.

Mistletoe Kiss Spell

"Oh, by gosh, by golly, it's time for mistletoe and holly // Fancy ties an' granny's pies an' folks stealin' a kiss or two."

———————————

A seasonal love spell to bring love in your year to come. Note: this spell is designed for consensual kisses only.

Gather:

- mistletoe sprig
- evergreen branches
- holly
- lipstick/chapstick
- dew/fresh fallen snow
- a rose petal

Assemble the plants them into an ornament you can hang.

Bless the lipstick/chapstick with dew or fresh-fallen snow, and a rose petal.

Solicit a consensual kiss from someone.

Kiss under the ornament, while wearing the lipstick/chapstick

If you don't have any mistletoe, you can always craft your own, or choose another plant with romantic connotations.

Note: under no circumstances, should you consume mistletoe. It can be deadly if swallowed. Handle with precaution.

'Over The Moon' Love Spell

———————

This spell was written to be particularly potent when the moon is full and/or in Taurus. However, it can be cast at any time that is available. This is a spell to attract general love and happiness to you.

Gather:

- o   rose quartz
- o   full moon water
- o   rosemary
- o   white thread, a sight of the full moon.

Perform during the full moon, if possible.

Kiss the rose quartz, then let it sit in the full moon water to charge with its energies.

Bind the rose quartz to the rosemary using the white thread, be sure to hold the quartz in front of, or above the moon in your line of sight as you bind it.

After, keep the finished spell near your bed, or as a charm on your person

Sweet and Salty Love Spell

This is a simple spell jar, made to attract kind people for relationships, but to also repel toxic or unkind people.

Gather:

- a jar to layer ingredients in
- a pink or white candle
- pink Himalayan rock salt - for defense against negativity
- white sugar - bring sweetness to the relationship
- rose petals - indicates romantic love

Layer ingredients in the jar. Charge with rose quartz, seal with melted candle wax and a kiss.

'Howl' Love Spell

A spell written to bring you courage, determination, and swiftness in going after one you want, romantically or platonically.

This spell does not guarantee any such confession will end well or protect against the pain of an injured heart, but merely arms you with the strength to face that being an outcome.

Gather:

- o a rosebud
- o two apple seeds
- o thyme
- o storm water
- o salt

First, conceal carefully the apple seeds within the petals of the rosebud, but take care to not separate the petals so much that they fall out.

Sprinkle the rose with thyme, salt, and the storm water, wait until it is dry. You may wish to dry it in between pages of a book.

Wrap the rosebud up if you wish, keep in your pocket as a charm for when you walk to them.

'We Met in a Dream' Spell

This is a spell for when you have a romantic dream, and it involves someone you know, or someone you would like to know, but when you wake and reality could not be farther from the dream. The intent of this spell is to bring the feelings experienced in the dream to fruition, and share them with the other person from the dream, known or unknown.

Gather:

- 3 apple seeds
- 3 rose buds
- a pinch of cinnamon
- a bay leaf
- a small box to contain them

Slip the apple seeds into the rose buds respectively. Two are for the other person's eyes, one for you. Kiss the one that represents you, and lay the bay leaf in the box.

Lay the rosebud that represents you on the bay leaf in the box. Place the other two eyes in the box on opposite sides of yours, sprinkle cinnamon only over them. Leave the box under your bed, in preparation for a future dream or after a dream that has already occurred.

Love Potion Tea

A potion, drink to bring you self-love, or strengthen the love you already share with another person.

This potion should not be given to another person without their consent, as it will not work, but also because it is illegal in most places to dose another person's food/drink with substances unknown to them.

Gather:

o   1 rose bud (washed)
o   1 tsp orange extract
o   1 cup black tea
o   dried orange slices
o   cinnamon to taste
o   cardamom to taste

Please consider the rosebud you are using, for if it is store-bought or grown with pesticides/preservatives, you may want to charge the tea-cup with it rather than consume it.

Steep the mixture 3-5 minutes, brew with intent in mind. Strain the ingredients out of the tea, or drink it lose-leaf if you prefer.

The Smolder" Love Spell

This is a little love spell/glamour, you can prepare beforehand, and then use by fluttering your eyelashes at someone.

If you wish to enchant a specific mascara or eye shadow, apply the charm to the outside of the makeup container instead of your eyes.

Gather:

- moon water
- rose petals
- strawberry leaves

Dab around eyes with the clean water, avoid direct contact with eyes.

Dab the water droplets with the rose petals and strawberry leaves. Apply to your eyes either the day/night of, or by makeup.

Note: use clean water you don't mind washing your face with to make the moon water, wash the rose petals and strawberry leaves.

Sexual Spells

Spell of Release

A simple spell for ending dry spells of romantic, creative, or other natures.

Gather:

- a bottle that seals
- soda water or alcohol
- a pink candle
- sea water
- a pinch of coconut shreddings
- a comfortable and private space

Light the pink candle in a safe space. In the bottle add an effect or herb that symbolizes the aspect you often need, rose for love, cocoa for lust, etc.

Combine with soda water or alcohol inside the bottle. Burn the coconut shreddings on the candle.

*Optional, use the climax of sexual or creative pleasure to charge the ingredients in the bottle.

Blow out the candle, gather the energies into the bottle.

Seal the bottle and attach burned coconut around the seal. Open when you need a dry spell to come to an end.

Seductive Words Glamour

A lipstick/chapstick glamour to make your words extra convincing, persuasive, or interesting to someone.

Gather:

- o chapstick/lipstick of your choice (though red would work best)
- o moon water
- o a basil leaf
- o a spring of rosemary

Soak the basil leaf and sprig of rosemary for an hour in the moon water.

Put a drop of moon water on the lipstick

If you want to make the spell for something/someone specific, add a sigil to the lipstick before you put it on.

Lust Spell

A spell to increase lust in oneself or a consenting individual.

Gather:

- a gourd
- a daisy
- sesame seeds
- vanilla extract

Cut the gourd in half, hollow it out on one side. In the hollow, place the daisy.

Sprinkle vanilla droplets and the sesame seeds over the daisy.

With your little finger, mix the ingredients clockwise in the hollow.

Mix a few times for a small increase in lust, many times for a large increase. If it is done too much, it can be reversed*

Put the gourd back together, and bury if possible. If not, dispose of it.

*The reversal spell is in the next chapter.

Strawberry Kiss Spell

A sweet spell to draw opportunities to bring sensuality into one's life. This spell is not designed to infringe upon any particular's consent.

Gather:

- o sugar
- o a strawberry
- o rose petals
- o a fireproof dish
- o matches

Hold the fruit in you palm, focusing intent and all related feelings into it.

When ready, kiss the strawberry, dip and roll in sugar.

Bearing no allergies, consume the fruit. If allergic, substitute with a fruit that is safe for you.

Cut the leaves from the strawberry. Burn the remaining leaves and rose petals in the dish.

For a more intense spell, sink teeth into the fruit on the kiss, bruise gently.

Anti-Love Spells

Unwanted Lover Spell
(Love Spell Reversal)

This is a spell meant to repel would-be romantic or sexual admirers, or to undo a love-spell gone wrong.

Gather:

- o the pieces/ingredients you used for the original love spell
- o A rose, burned to ash
- o Something representative of the person pursuing you, a picture perhaps.

Salt lightly and burn what you can.

Mix these things together, then pour out into a little pile of ashes on the front or back step. Chant:

"Get the fuck out of my life
I do not like you
You are causing me strife
Shove off, creep."

Sweep the ashes away into the wind with a broom. (Outdoors would be preferable). Sweep it away into the wind.

No Love Lost Spell

A spell to prevent developing feelings for someone, or to remove the affection

Gather:

- o rose
- o burning plate
- o matches
- o sign of the person
- o half an apple & seeds

Choose either soft pink roses or red, depending on the nature of the feelings.

Slice the apple in half. Consume one half.

Gouge the seeds out, mix the seeds with the rose petals. Burn the mixture to ashes.

Bury the other half of the apple in the ground, and nothing will grow there.

Smear ashes on the back doorstep, or scatter in the wind.

Anti-Lust Spell
(Or Lust Spell Reversal)

A spell to lower lust in oneself or a consenting individual

Gather:

- a gourd
- a daisy
- salt
- sesame seeds
- vanilla

Cut the gourd in half, hollow it out.

In the hollow, place a daisy.

Sprinkle vanilla and sesame seeds over the daisy. Pluck out the petals.

Burn and salt the daisy.

Put the gourd back together, and bury if possible. If not, dispose of it.

Platonic Love / Friendship Spells

Friendship Fastening Spell

A consensual binding spell for friends, inspired by traditional hand-fasting ceremonies. The intent is to support and celebrate a friendship, not bind a person to you forever. This spell is to be done with both parties present.

Gather:

- o strawberry leaves
- o yellow string
- o a white candle
- o representative objects of each friend involved

Using the yellow string, wrap the representative objects together with the strawberry leaves between them. Take turns wrapping the object with the string.

Chant while wrapping:

"With your hands and mine

Through this string we entwine

Secure a friendship forever fine."

Seal the knot with white wax.

Friendship/Conversation Attraction Spell

Find something that represents yourself, preferably small.

Eat some strawberries while you say this chant:

> *"With friendship on my mouth, I know*
>
> *I attract friends and conversation*
>
> *These seeds I plant, discourse I sow*
>
> *This spell will build my friendship's foundation."*

Save some of the seeds, place them, the object that represents you, and some rosemary in an envelope or sachet. Keep it in your pocket for when you are in the same area as the people you want to be friends with.

Contagious Laughter Spell

A spell to bring happiness to your loved ones and friends

Gather:

- o morning dew
- o citrine
- o rose quartz
- o vanilla
- o a sachet
- o pink ribbon

Place crystals in the sachet, anoint with morning dew

Hold the bag and charge it with good feelings, laughter, etc.

Place a drop of vanilla on each end of the ribbon

Tie the bag with the ribbon, seal with a kiss.

Give it to the person, or attach something of theirs to the bag.

A Spell to Let Emotions/Empathy Flow Between Two People

If it's in your practice to do so, cast a circle big enough for the two of you to sit across from one another, with two bowls in between, invoke your deities, cleanse, etc. Cleanse and charge the items you will be using. This spell is best done outside in the grass, under the moon.

Gather:

- two blue candles
- a small representative objective of each person
- moon water
- thyme
- bay leaf
- lemon

Sit opposite your friend. Light the two blue candles between you.

Take something of hers and something of yours, a ring or a bracelet perhaps. Pour the moon water into the empath's bowl.

Mix in herbs of thyme, bay leaf, and lemon. Fill your bowl almost to the brim. Cup your hands in the water and chant as you pour the handfuls of water into your friend's bowl, over their hands, sitting in their bowl:

"My bowl overflows,
While yours like a sieve.
What the empath knows
From this night on, I give."

Have them wash their hands in the water accumulating in their bowl.

"I unburden from your mind
The weight of others hearts
Our efforts combined,
I share your knowledge in part."

Repeat the chants until you have emptied half of what you had into their bowl. Blow out the candles, close the circle, thank your gods, etc. Bottle up the water from each bowl and keep it in your rooms.

When alone and you feel the bond is wearing thin, repeat the chant and sprinkle a little water over your token.

When together, wear the items at the same time and tell her about the things you feel, and have her respond to these things. End the exchange with this chant:

> *"Burden no more, when it is shared*
> *Through the bond of us two paired."*

Rose Quartz Altruistic Love Spell

A spell to encourage unconditional and altruistic love for humanity and Earth, and give an air of approachable serenity.

Gather:

- o straw
- o maple leaf
- o chocolate
- o a piece of rose quartz

Pair the wrapped chocolate and rose quartz together

Wrap inside a maple leaf

Tie with straw and seal with a kiss.

Charge the package with your love for your fellows.

Charge under the moon light

When it's ready, unwrap the maple leaf.

Consume the chocolate and keep the quartz on you as a charm.

For Help with Relationships

A Spell to Help Someone See Your Feelings

Write a letter detailing your feelings and roll it up. Seal something inside the letter, something that represents the person.

Light a blue candle, and wait until the flame burns strong. Chant, burning the letter:

"Know my feelings, how you have snubbed me by the blue candle that burns: to this gain clarity."

Blow out the candle.

Stay with Me Spell

This is a spell to strengthen your bond with someone.

Carve the candle with both of your names, one of either side. Tie a string around the candle, and light the orange candle.

Chant:

"I tie this knot, with a string, long
to keep our communication strong.
By this candle's orange hue,
I preserve the relation between us two."

Wait until the wax melts over the string.
Blow out the candle, and preserve the string in
your room.

Bring Us Closer Spell

Carve the person's name into a candle, and
yours on the other side.

Chant:

"With the power of our names

I bring our paths to intertwine

Through this burning flame

To learn of you is my design."

Let the candle burn all the way through, or
at least until it has burned through both
names. Do not leave the candle unattended.

Sweeten Your Feelings Jar Spell

A jar spell to sweeten the bond you share with someone.

Gather:

- o   A representative object of you
- o   A representative object of them
- o   Lemon seeds
- o   Honey
- o   sugar
- o   A candle

Find a representative object of you and the person, it should be small enough to fit in the jar. Mix the ingredients together in the jar. Optional, light a yellow/orange/pink candle, depending on the nature of the relationship. Put the representative object in the jar.

Chant:

"Sweet as sugar, by this honeyed spell, only in nectarous feelings our bond shall dwell puckered lips, our love shall never be sour, from these seeds sweeter feelings flower."

Seal with wax. To dispose/break the spell: rinse the mixture out of the jar, cleanse and empty jar.

Long Distance Spell

You will need four things. Two things from you, two things from your friend. Pair one of your things with one of theirs. Tie each pair together with a white thread.

Place them by a white candle, on either side. Sprinkle the candle with thyme, strawberry, and lemon balm.

Chant:

"Through hardship and distance
and all other resistance
our bond will not be neglected
we will remain connected
by candle and herb I bless these charms
by them, our bond comes to no harm."

Let the charms charge by the candle, and after the spell is done give your friend the other charm.

'My Jolly Sailor Bold' Love Spell

A sea witch's spell for drawing in a lover, or draw one back from leaving often.

Gather:

- o   pink sea salt
- o   a fishnet stocking
- o   pyrite
- o   lemon peel
- o   sea-water
- o   a jar
- o   a blue and a pink candle
- o   a coin

Play, or sing along to the shanty "my jolly sailor bold".

Light the two candles on either side of the jar. Fill the jar with pink sea salt and lemon peel. Bury the coin, place the pyrite in the jar.

*"My heart is pierced by Cupid,
I disdain all glittering gold,*

*There is nothing that can console me
but my jolly sailor bold."*

Fill the jar with the seawater, and cover the bottle with the fishnet, tie off. Seal the jar with a kiss and the two kinds of wax.

Nostalgia Spell

This is a spell designed to share your nostalgia for specific memories with someone else, and remind them of the memories.

- o Gather:
- o Rue
- o Rosemary
- o Photos
- o A box

If you share photos with that person, print them out. This is to help you visualize those old memories and bring them into the present.

Then gather any mementos, or things you still have from that person, and put them in a box.

Place a sprig of rosemary, and if you have it, some rue flowers in the box. Shake gently and say/think,

"Remember, remember that I do

The days of us, and pleasantly too.

Now by rosemary sprig and bud of rue,

Please come to remember these things too."

Hide the box under your bed. If you feel you need to do it again, try only to do it once a week.

Dispose of the box when you're ready.

Tiny Truth Spell

This is a spell to learn the truth from one question from one person.

Gather:

- o Paper
- o candle

Write your question and the person's name on the paper. Light the candle, and as you burn it, chant softly:

"Whisper once your word of truth

Just one answer I wish to know

Bring to me through tongue and tooth

I plant the seed and truth I'll sow."

Blow out the candle.

Rekindling Spell

First find a box of matches that you'll use. Put a rose petal in the box, or some rose quartz, and leave it overnight under the moonlight to charge with loving energy. If you need to use a lighter instead, leave it in a jacket or pants pocket with the rose petals or quartz, same deal with the moonlight.

Find moment to light a literal fire between you, whether it is a campfire, or maybe you sit down to dinner and decide to have a candlelit meal for once. You can sit across or next to him, as long as you're generally pointed to the candle.

Use the prepared matches/lighter to light the fire. Have a friendly conversation over the fire. Feel the fire's energy filling up your relationship.

Drop the word "spark" into the conversation casually. This is the only word you will need for the incantation, and you only need to say it once. Let the conversation last as long as it can.

Put the fire/candle out safely, but try to keep the fire's energy in mind. It does not go out with the flame if you don't let it. You can do this spell more than once if you like, but try to space it out.

Show Me Your Love Spell

_____

A spell to help people more easily express their feelings to one another.

Gather:

- o   rose petals
- o   dill
- o   white candle

Dry some rose petals and crush them, add dill. Put a little in your pillowcase.

Make a little circle out of the rest of the herbs, put the candle in the center. Burn it and chant:

"By rosemary and dill this spell starts
Draw me closer and show your cares
As I've held you in my arms
And you hold me in your heart."

Save the herbs in a bag. If the spell becomes too much, so you can salt and burn them to end it.

Stop Ignoring Me Spell

Place a small pinch of dill, and a fragment of a rose petal under your tongue. Concentrate on the intention "open your mouth, open your heart" for a little while.

Give him a kiss on the cheek.

then go into the bathroom alone. chant/think:

"Open your mouth, let me see your heart

Spill the feelings that are keeping us apart."

as you rinse the herbs out of your mouth with water, imagine his opening up to you.

repeat if you like, but no more than twice a day.

Contact Spell

If your practice calls for it, invoke your corresponding deities/elements/planets, cast a circle, etc. This is optional.

Draw the sign of mercury and charge it. Place a shallow bowl over the sign, place your phone opposite you, near the bowl.

Write your and the person's number on separate pieces of paper. If you have a piece of clear quartz (preferably cleansed/charged but no big deal if it isn't) rub it over the numbers, three times each, then place it in the bowl. If you have no quartz, use your finger. Chant, say, sing or think:

"Any words you have waiting for me,

Be brought to the front of your mind

Please, from me, the powers that be,

Lead my friend, that he should find

Our correspondence is long overdue,

Spark a dialogue, to me from you!"

After, take the papers and burn them, or tear them up into small pieces. Mix in the bowl, mix in your caraway and dill. Leave by the window, or sprinkle outside in the wind, in the direction of that person's house.

Of course, there is a mundane method as well, simply call or text them yourself. I know that option is scarier, but results are 100% quicker, so I'm going to include a quick little courage spell: take a pinch of basil, hold it to your heart and repeat the things you want to say to the person, until you feel a bit stronger. Place the basil under your tongue, drink some water and text/call them.

Rose Romance Spell

A spell to aid romance for couples that don't connect in all the conventional ways

Gather: a whole peach, rose quartz, a normal rock, and one of the items below that corresponds to what you feel is missing from the relationship.

dill = communication

vanilla = lust

poppy seeds = romance

cumin = fidelity

coconut = chastity

bluebell = trust

cypress = peace

Cut the peach in half, take the pit out.

Put the rose quartz and the normal rock where the pit was

Sprinkle your chosen ingredient over the inside of the peach.

Close up the peach.

Bury the peach. Keep the pit.

For Sour
Relationships

'What Kind of Man Loves Like This' Spell

A spell to help release yourself from a bad relationship in your life

Gather:

- o a red and a blue candle
- o half an apple
- o coffee grounds
- o pepper
- o salt
- o pine needles
- o representation of the person you wish to distance yourself from

Light the candle, and take half the apple, which represents the rotting relationship.

Bury the coffee, pepper, salt, pine needles, the banishing elements, and the representative object, in the core of the apple half. Burn the whole thing with the red and blue candle(s).

As it burns, feel the bonds of the relationship dissolve away

Dispose of the burned apple somewhere safe.

Know What You Have Done Spell

This is a spell to let the person know how they are affecting you negatively, so that they may gain a new perspective on

Find a picture of the two of you, and roll it up with some rosemary inside, fresh or dried, whichever is easier to procure. Tie it with string, and light a black or white candle. Burn the rolled picture.

Chant:

> *"Wasted friendship, wasted years,*
>
> *Know and feel these wasted tears.*
>
> *By broken bond and rosemary*
>
> *Know, and regret what*
>
> *you have done to me."*

Lapis Water Binding

A spell to bind and banish those to a place they cannot travel from

Gather:

- lapis lazuli
- sea salt water
- a rock or something heavy as an anchor
- black thread

Create one taglock for the person/thing you are binding.

Create the other taglock, for the part of yourself that has been affected by the person/thing. This is to bind the affect-or and the affected area away together.

Mix the sea salt and the water, bind the taglocks and the anchor with black thread.

Drown the bound objects, chant the above quote if you like.

You can put the lapis lazuli in the water during this enchantment, but know it is a water-soluble stone. Alternatively, you can hold it over the bowl for the spell.

Cold Shoulder Spell

A spell for pushing two people apart.

Find a picture of the two of them, preferably printed out, on something flimsy, like paper. Place the picture in a box you don't mind getting wet. Get some ice, and chip it up into small pieces.

Chant:

> *"Sharp as ice and just as cold,*
>
> *I break the bond these two hold.*
>
> *With ice, now, let friendship freeze,*
>
> *Let these two become enemies."*

Create a line/wall of ice between the two in the picture, down the middle. Close the box and let the ice melt and soak the picture, slowly blurring the ink and weakening the paper. Wait till the ice is all melted, and then reapply and repeat this step as many times as you feel necessary. Or until the picture is destroyed

Tongue Tying Spell

A spell for binding and unwanted flirter.

Find something that represents his mouth, a drawing or a picture, anything. Write the names of the girls you don't want him to talk to on the back. Bind with black thread, and then burn it over a black candle.

Chant:

"Your tongue is tied, it belongs to me

I have your voice but it is only lip service.

To flirt with other girls you won't be free.

By black thread and candle,

Let this spell preserve us."

Keep the ashes in an envelope.

Wrapped Around Your Finger
- A Binding Spell

A spell for binding and many unwanted flirters.

Take one glove from a pair the person has worn. Write the names of the people who flirt and write them down, slip them inside each of the fingers of the gloves. Bind each of the fingers with black thread/string. Seal each knot with the wax from a black candle, and after each finger, chant:

"Give me your hands,
which you promised to me

I have your voice
but it is only lip service.

To exchange flirts
with others you won't be free.

By black thread,
let this spell preserve us."

Bind it tight as you can with the thread, seal with black thread. Keep in a box out of sight.

To Bind A Stalker Spell:

Use a picture of them, or an effect of theirs, and begin tying it up with black string or thread.

"I restrict you, you won't bother me

Your words won't touch my mind

Of this spell you won't be free

Until this thread unbinds."

Repeat the chant until you have covered the entire thing with the black string/thread, make sure you cannot see any bit of the original object.

Self Love

Rose Bath Spell

A simple bath ritual of roses and milk to gather love and beauty

Gather:

- o   dried milk
- o   epsom salts
- o   rose petals
- o   sliced strawberries

Fill a bath with hot water, mix 1 ½ cups dried milk into the hot water

Dissolve epsom salts in the water and stir.

Sprinkle the rose petals over the top of the bath

Soak in the bath, absorbing its soft warm energies.

Eat the strawberry slices. Each bite leaves loving words in your mouth.

Moon Glamour

A glamour to feel confident and beautiful, even when nervous and self-conscious

Gather:

- quartz
- a white candle
- a pink ribbon
- a flower
- orange
- thyme

Tie the ribbon around the candle.

Dress the candle with the flower, orange peel, and thyme.

Burn the candle, chant,

"By the light of the moon".

Blow out the candle, pass the quartz through the smoke.

Tie the quartz with the ribbon and keep on your person as a charm.

Use the charm as needed.

'On Fire' Confidence Spell

A candle spell for self-confidence, fearlessness and boldness

Gather:

- o celery leaves
- o thyme
- o red ribbon
- o an orange candle

Wrap the candle with the red ribbon.

Light the candle.

Burn leaves and thyme in the flame.

Concentrate on absorbing the vibrant energy from the candle.

When satisfied, blow the candle out.

Self Care – Habits

Princess Sleep Spell

A pillow spell for sleeping well with pleasant dreams

Gather:

- o   pillow
- o   sachet
- o   lavender or chamomile
- o   cucumber peel

Combine the cucumber peel and lavender/chamomile in the sachet

Keep the sachet inside your pillowcase, amethyst under the pillow

Place amethyst under bed during your sleep.

Place amethyst under pillow during the day, or when not sleeping.

Spell to Help Break Bad Habits

A spell that mixes mundane methods with magic to help break bad habits

Gather:

- black thread
- bay leaf
- a different, healthy habit you want to replace it with

Identify what brings the habit on: boredom, convenience, etc.

Bind it with the black thread.

Burn the bay leaf and sprinkle the ashes over the new habit

Keep the objects near one another, to remind you to opt for the good habit over the bad one.

Healthy Eating Spell

A spell to aid in the eating foods for a healthy diet, neither too little nor too much.

Gather:

- o moon water
- o salt
- o a cinnamon stick
- o an apple

Combine salt and moon water.

Cut the apple in half, leave half in the salt/moon water.

Leave the cinnamon stick on top of the apple in the water.

Eat the other half of the apple.

Dry out the cinnamon stick, hang it in front of your food cabinet/fridge.

Stuffed Animal Sleep Spell

A spell for keeping negativity out of dreams, whether it's pain, difficult subjects, or people that hurt you.

Gather:

- o a pillow or stuffed animal
- o apple seeds
- o dried lavender
- o rosemary

Charge the herbs under the moonlight.

Open up the pillow, place the herbs inside.

Stitch the pillow back up. Keep the pillow on the bed when you sleep.

Facewash Spell

A simple spell to promote beautiful or healthy skin.

Gather:

- o a blue candle
- o rose quartz
- o facewash of choice
- o a mirror

Leave the rose quartz to charge the facewash of choice while not using it.

When you go to wash your face, light the candle nearby.

Anoint the mirror with a drop of wax.

Use the facewash as you would normally, wash and rinse your face.

Pat your face dry and blow out the candle.

Remove wax from the mirror, leave rose quartz to charge facewash.

Restarting Spell

A ritual for fresh starts, to remove old energies, and invite new ones in

To be done at the end of the year, midnights, or the end of each month

Gather:

- o a white candle
- o salt
- o two pages
- o a fire-safe surface

Write about, or in a sigil, represent the aspects you want to shake off.

On the second page, write the things you wish to usher in.

Place the positive one under the candle, and draw a circle of salt around the candle. Burn the negative note.

If you plan to repeat the ritual, use the back of the positive note to collect the negativities for when you burn it later.

To do as a group ritual, arrange the candles in a circle or mark all pages with a unifying sigil.

Self Care – Emotional

Bubble Your Feelings Spell

A spell to bubble feelings that are causing you harm, such as unrequited love

Gather:

- o a pearl
- o an object that represents your feelings
- o a box
- o a white candle.

If you do not have a pearl, use clear quartz or glass.

Gather up your feelings and push them onto the object. Box the object up.

Drip white wax onto the opening of the box, sealing it.

Draw a circle in the air around the box with the pearl.

It is finished. It will not bother you until you unbubble it.

This can be done without an object, only with thought, but it is harder to accomplish them.

Reflected Illusion Glamour

A glamour to blend in, or make something less noticeable

Gather:

- o water
- o sea salt
- o a mirror
- o daisy petals

On the surface on the mirror, mix the water and sea salt

Chant:

"Reflected by the water,

Hidden by the light."

Dip the daisy petals into the water

Use the petals to dab the water on what you wish to hide

Clear Speaking Glamour

A spell to aid with speaking clearly, and get your point across.

Gather:

- lipstick/chapstick of your choice
- basil
- morning dew
- violet petals

Ensure the lipstick/chapstick is completely closed.

Go over the outside of the container with the dew and the basil.

Let them charge the balm.

Wipe them off, apply the balm. Kiss the violet to start the spell.

No Light, No Light

A spell to figure out what you or another need to say someone, and to help you say, be it an apology or a confession.

Gather:

- rosemary
- dill
- two blue candles

Perform on or by "the empty space in" your bed, at night.

Carve your name in one candle, the other person's name on the other.

Dress your representative candle with dill and rosemary

Light the other person's candle first, and let it burn down a little. Then use it to light your candle

Blow out the candles, go to bed.

Play the song while you perform the ritual, dance and sing along if you like.

The answer will start to form after that morning, in the things you say to other people, but not that person.

What the Water Said Spell

A spell to help ease those overburdened by worries/anxieties they can't control. Not a substitute for trained help

Gather:

- o stones
- o lavender
- o sea salt
- o coriander

Mix herbs in the water, a tub or a sink.

Play the song while you perform the ritual, dance and sing along if you like.

For each issue/burden, create a representing sigil and draw it on a rock with something biodegradable.

If you are not willing to take a bath, fill a sink with water and simply submerge your hands instead.

Submerge as much of yourself as is comfortable (not your face). Think on the things that are holding you down. Each time you bring your head/hands up, drop one of the rocks. Do this until you hold none.

Remain in the water a moment, feeling the weightlessness it gives you.

Take the rocks to a pond and leave them underwater.

Self Love Bath Ritual

For this ritual, gather a bath bomb, rose quartz, vanilla scented soap, a red candle, and if you're of age, wine of choice.

Light the red candle, arrange the rose quartz as you like. Use the vanilla soap to cleanse negative energies away.

Add the bath bomb, soak in the tub and bring in new, calm energies. Enjoy the bath with your drink of choice.

Lover by Lover Spell

A spell for when you feel you've been messing up and need a fresh start and reassurance.

Best performed outside, under clouds, or near your bed, a pair of shoes.

Gather:

- o black candle
- o red candle
- o crossroads dirt/stones
- o something to represent your heart and something for the soul

Light the candles, one in front of each shoe.

Place the heart and soul pieces, one in each shoe.

Rub crossroads dirt on the bottom of each shoe.

Blow out the candles

Let the shoes sit under you bed for the night.

Play the song while you perform the ritual, dance and sing along if you like.

Held By the Ocean

A bath spell for comfort and assurance in one's self.

Perform on a night that the moon is out, in any phase that you can see.

Gather:

- o a few drops of ocean water
- o sugar
- o rosemary
- o lavender
- o thyme
- o two mirrors, facing each other
- o a white candle between them

Let the moonlight shine onto the bathwater and charge before you get in. If you have no window for moonlight, charge some moon water beforehand and pour that in the bath.

Mix in sugar, lavender, rosemary and thyme. Light the candle, listen to the song. Bathe until the water is cold.

Feel the water support you and strengthen your heart.

Faint Heart Glamour

A glamour intended to bring you courage and make you feel invincible.

Gather:

- o a shiny mirror by a sunny window
- o a flower crown

Preferably make the crown of basil, thyme, pennyroyal, thistle, or carnations. However, any flowers will do.

Hang the flower crown on the mirror and apply your usual makeup routine/brush your hair while looking at your reflection through the crown.

When you are finished with your routine, turn to the sunlight, bathe in its warmth and envision that it is turning you to gold.

Wear the flower crown after if you like.

Shine Like the Sun

A spell that uses the shine of sunlight to reveal inner and outer beauty.

Gather:

- o lemon juice
- o a comb
- o a mirror
- o a pink or yellow candle

Perform spell early in the morning, sit before the sun as it rises.

Light the candle before you, placed on top of the mirror. Brush your hair, and comb lemon juice through it.

Burn any strands that come out while brushing it in the candle.

Take care not to burn yourself, and chant

"Eyes bright as my laugh and hair to match

By the fierce sun, I keep the light I catch!"

Blow out the candle.

Friendship/Conversation Attraction Spell:

Gather:

- representative object
- strawberries
- rosemary
- envelope/sachet

Find something that represents yourself, preferably small.

Eat some strawberries while you say this chant:

"With friendship on my mouth, I know

I attract friends and conversation.

These seeds I plant, discourse I sow

This spell will draw my friendship's foundation."

Save some of the seeds, place them, the object that represents you, and some rosemary in an envelope/sachet. Keep it in your pocket for when you are in the same area as the people you want to be friends with.

Sapphire Insecurity Spell

A spell, to help when one feels small or useless, overwhelmed and alone

Gather:

- o a sapphire or similar stone
- o ivy
- o white candle

Place the white candle on an ivy leaf.

Embed the candle with the stone, and light the candle.

Speak your insecurities over the candle.

Blow out the candle when ready.

Hurricane Hurt Spell

A spell for when things can't hurt any worse, to turn your pain into invincibility.

Gather:

- clover
- basil
- pine needles
- grass
- lilac
- rosemary

A bowl or rain water.

Steep the herbs in the bowl of rainwater.

Perform in the rain, or the shower.

Sprinkle with rainwater over your head. Feel the cool water becoming a shield over your skin. It is not cold, it is numb.

Glow Like the Moon

A spell to recapture youth and beauty with the gentleness of the moon's glow.

Gather:

- o a white or pink candle
- o full moon water
- o cosmetics or face lotion

Light your candle, a plain one or a pink one. Do at night, look up at the mostly full moon.

Anoint the cosmetics or face lotion with the full moon water.

Apply the cosmetics or face lotion, then speak:

"Moon, bright and full, grant me your glow

Bring back the beauty that I used to know."

Bask in the moonlight for a little while, until you feel it is done.

Blow out your candle.

Venus Transformation Glamour

A glamour to transform the perceptions of the ordinary to beautiful and powerful.

If you want to use a wand or similar tool, feel free.

Gather:

- o almond
- o apricot
- o holly
- o daisy

With each the almond, apricot, and holly trace a circle in the air around yourself, encircling yourself with their power

Chant,

"By the power and influence of Venus!"

Wear the daisy in your hair

Go feel pretty and powerful.

Stars Guide Me Home Spell

A celestial spell to bring home those that are lost, in a physical or emotional sense, for what is lost and or when you need a sense of direction in your life

Gather:

- o   a sight of Polaris
- o   a compass
- o   dandelion
- o   a bay leaf

Gently invoke the influence of Polaris, the North Star using its symbol.

Draw the symbol on the compass

Under the starlight, burn the dandelion and bay leaf

Rub the ash on the compass.

Keep the compass as a charm, over something of yours, or something of the one you want to come home.

Wait for signs of guidance from Polaris using the compass.

Mermaid Singing Glamour

A glamour to help your singing voice be like a mermaid's.

Gather:

- a seashell
- full moon or ocean water
- a pinch of glitter
- a necklace chain
- a song that makes you confident in your singing voice

Mix the water with the glitter. Rinse the seashell in the water.

Play the song and sing along with it as you mix the water clockwise.

When the song is over, dry it out and make it into a necklace.

Wear the necklace when you feel you need a boost with your singing voice.

Amethyst Empowerment Spell

A spell to help bring about self-empowerment.

Gather:

- thistle
- amethyst
- cascarilla powder

Prepare the cascarilla powder.

Grind up the thistle and mix it in.

Create a circle with the powder.

Charge the amethyst within the circle.

Take it and the comfort of the ring with you wherever you go.

Spell for the Tide-Waiter

A charm to bring patience to the owner, or influence an area.

Gather:

- a bowl of seawater
- twine
- almond
- lavender
- an orange

Bundle lavender together, tie together with twine and tie hook.

Prepare seawater with orange. Soak thoroughly.

Dip the lavender in the water three times, each waiting for the water to still.

Tie the almond as part of the bundle.

Hang in the respective home.

Peridot Personal Growth Spell

A spell for personal growth.

Gather:

- o   peridot or similar stone
- o   green candle
- o   periwinkle

Wrap the candle with the periwinkle vine.

Embed the candle with the stone, and light the candle.

Write an affirmation of what you want to change/grow in, and chant it.

Blow out the candle when you're done with the affirmation.

Determination Spell

_____

A spell to fill you with determination to do kind things, be better, or achieve a goal.

Gather:

- aventurine
- stormwater
- thyme
- a jar
- a green candle

Fill the jar with aventurine and thyme.

Melt a green candle to seal it.

Let the jar rest overnight in a bowl of stormwater.

Keep the jar on you as a charm to help you with determination and kindness.

Mermaid's Breath Spell

A spell for the ability to survive in emotional or situational circumstances a bit out of your depth or comfort zone, like a fish out of water.

Gather:

- o   sea water
- o   stormwater
- o   aventurine
- o   a seashell
- o   a blue candle

Embed the candle with the aventurine and light it. Mix the sea and storm water, and fill the seashell with it. Blow the candle out and pass the seashell through the smoke.

Chant:

" Aquea pulmonem there:

Come swifter than winds over the sea

Demersi sunt in aere,

Tenere spiritum, la spiritus to me."

Place the seashell somewhere safe to hold the water until the spell is over.

Peaceful Space Spell

A spell to promote tranquility and good feelings in an environment

Gather:

- lavender
- myrtle
- vanilla extract
- violets
- white ribbon

Braid the stems of the plants together, tie at the end with ribbon.

Set bouquet out in the sunlight to dry completely.

Hang above the front door of the space you wish to enchant.

Bless the frame of the door and the four corners of the room with vanilla.

For each thought/worry you have, pluck a needle off the rosemary.

Arrange the needles around the rose quartz.

Each time you put a needle down, remind yourself it's just a thought.

When you are done, sprinkle the thyme over it and leave it alone for a while.

Sweep up the herbs and take the rose quartz with you.

'On Your Toes' Spell

———————

A glamour to allow one the grace to navigate difficult situations.

Gather:

- o   a pair of shoes
- o   morning dew
- o   vervain or rosemary
- o   pink thread

Sew a small patch containing the vervain into some part of the shoe.

Bless the toes of the shoes with the morning dew.

With the thread, create an 'x' on the heels, and ground the heel.

Wear the shoes in times of delicate situations.

Soft Shores Bath Spell

_____

A calming bath spell for peace and tranquility in one's life and energy

Gather:

- seawater
- a shell
- pink salt
- soap
- a sprig of rosemary
- a comb

If you wish to, invoke Aphrodite's influence, offer her the shell.

Rinse and comb your hair with the sea water.

Prepare the bath with the pink salt and soap.

Float the sprig of rosemary on the water.

Be careful not to sink the rosemary as you soak in the bath.

Comb hair and keep the water as calm, take as long as you need

If you invoked her influence, thank Aphrodite and drain the bath.

Jar Spell for Clarity

A simple springtime spell for emotional/mental clarity, and wisdom.

Gather:

- o raspberry
- o amethyst
- o bay leaf
- o sage
- o sunflower seeds or petals

In a bowl, crush the raspberry. Soak the opening of the jar in the juice.

Fill the jar with dried bay leaf, sage, and sunflower seeds.

Seal the jar carefully with wax of the color most calming to you.

Charge with amethyst as needed, shake to invoke.

Calcified Heart Spell

A spell to protect your emotions // hold weak moments until they can be private

Gather:

- o clay
- o a bruised peach
- o eggshell
- o rose
- o sea salt

Grind the eggshell, rose, and sea salt together. Mix with the clay.

Take the pit out of the peach to keep as a charm.

Cover the peach with the clay, then bury the peach.

Your heart will be protected, but it will still be soft on the inside.

Sugar & Spice Prosperity Jar Spell

A jar spell to grant general prosperity and draw in good things.

Light a white candle.

Gather and layer in a jar:

- o Dried rose petals - for kind feelings in life
- o Cinnamon - wealth and prosperity
- o White sugar - to bring good natured things to you
- o Pink Himalayan rock salt - for defense against negativity
- o Dried coffee grounds - for motivation and catalyst

Charge with rose quartz or sunlight, seal with a kiss and the white wax.

Sea of Tears Jar Spell

A jar spell to help keep you afloat in your sadness.

Gather:

- two jars of different sizes one that can easily fit inside the other
- blue glitter
- moon water
- a taglock

Prepare the first jar with the taglock inside. Seal carefully so no water can get inside

Fill the second jar with the moon water and blue glitter.

Put the smaller jar inside, and seal the smaller bottle in the larger bottle

Shake gently when sad, and each time, when the small jar rises to the top, so do your emotions

The water may represent tears, but they are healing in their own way.

Just a Thought Spell

A spell to help calm you down from the little things and stray thoughts that worry you.

Gather:

- rose quartz
- rosemary
- thyme

Listen to the song while you perform the spell.

For each thought/worry you have, pluck a needle off the branch of rosemary. Arrange the needles around the rose quartz.

Each time you put a needle down, remind yourself it's just a thought. When you are done, sprinkle the thyme over it and leave it alone until you're ready.

Sweep up the herbs and take the rose quartz with you, burn the herbs.

Queen of Peace

A spell for when there is too much pain and turmoil to bear.

Perform preferably during the setting sun. Night is good too.

Gather:

- paper
- pine cone bits
- chamomile
- coffee grounds

Create a small, bio-degradable "boat". Locate a pond you can leave it in.

On the "boat", inscribe all your troubles, everything that is plaguing your mind. List merely their names or write paragraphs about them, your choice.

Sprinkle the boat with pine cone bits, chamomile, and coffee grounds.

Place it in the water, and let it float away. As it disappears, let your troubles go with it.

"Just Fuck Me Up" Spell

This is a "universe I'm ready to take five curveballs right now for the assurance it will all end well. Just fuck me up right now" spell.

Gather:

- o tarot cards
- o five things that symbolize yourself and your situation
- o five candles
- o bay leaf
- o coffee grounds
- o basil
- o storm water

Perform in as much darkness as you are comfortable with.

Create a pentagram, and at each point place a token of something that represents a key aspect of your personality.

Light a corresponding candle by each.

With the bay leaf, coffee ground, and basil, combine into a mixture. Burn a pinch of the mixture over each candle.

Speak of, or meditate on the subject of each representative object, and how it has been hindering you. Think on the ways it may have to get worse before it can get better.

Select tower and chariot cards from the deck, fan them out and place them in the center.

Utter the incantation to the universe once you have gathered all the energies and intents you need, "just fuck me up"

Extinguish the candles one by one using the storm water.

Cotton Candy Clouds

———————

A spell to create a soft, sweet, calming environment for self care and self love.

Gather:

- o sugar
- o chamomile
- o celestite or preferred crystal
- o white candle

Sprinkle sugar and chamomile into the candle. Light the candle and charge the desired crystal with it. Place the crystal in the area you wish to promote a caring environment.

Recharge the crystal as needed.

Healing Spells

Queen of Hearts
Moving Up Spell

A spell for when you leave a bad relationship, to help you find a better one than you had before.

Gather:

- a joker card
- choose at least one between the king/queen
- jack of hearts card
- a black and a red candle
- ivy

List the bad qualities of your last relationship on the joker card.

Listen the qualities you hope to find in someone new on the king, queen, jack cards, according to the gender(s) you are attracted to.

Group the three candles together, wrap them together with the ivy.

Burn the joker card on the black candle for banishment.

Burn the king/queen/joker card on the red candle for love.

Dog Days Are Over Ritual

———————

A potion to bring happy days and self love.

Gather:

- coffee
- rose quartz
- citrine
- lavender
- cinnamon
- maple

Make coffee to your taste, add the tiniest bits of lavender, cinnamon, or maple.

Kiss the pieces of rose quartz and citrine when you finish the drink.

Hide the rose quartz and citrine behind corners in your room and under your bed

Wash the cup. Let it go.

Alexandrite Separating Spell

A spell to separate toxicity from a person, whether it is a toxic situation, person, or behavior.

Gather:

- o a representative object of the person
- o one for their toxic situation
- o white thread
- o red wax
- o a knife
- o a piece of alexandrite

Meld the two objects together with red wax.

After it has set, cut the pieces apart, and bind each separately with white thread.

Leave the two pieces next to each other, with the alexandrite in between the, creating a barrier.

Rose Quartz Healing Tears

A spell to help heal what is hurt emotionally.

Gather:

- o full moon water
- o a piece of rose quartz
- o pink salt
- o lemon balm

Mix the pink salt and lemon balm into the moon water. Let it soak.

Dip the rose quartz into the water.

Let the water from the wet rose quartz drip onto your skin, like tears.

Let it work. Let it out. Things often hurt before they can heal.

How Big, How Blue

A spell for when you're changing, and it's time to become a new person.

Gather:

- o a white candle
- o a body of water
- o a skyline
- o objects that represent the person you wish to become

Light the candle, carry it.

To the best of your ability, wade into the water, in the proper attire.

Let yourself sink as far into the water as you are comfortable, underneath for a second, but only if you can.

Douse the candle in the water. Rise and leave your old self in the water. Take up your new self in the skyline.

Opal Mending Spell

A spell to help heal a bond between two people who don't always get along.

Gather:

- o   a pearl
- o   amethyst
- o   a yellow candle
- o   lavender
- o   ivy
- o   mint

Wrap the candle with the ivy. Embed the pearl and amethyst into the candle.

Burn the lavender and mint in the candle.

As it burns, text, call, or contact the person you want to mend your bond with.

Don't rush things, it doesn't need to heal all at once. The candle can be relit many times, for as many calls as you need.

Faded Memory Spell

A spell to help fade embarrassing memories that are uncomfortable to revisit.

Gather:

- o rosemary
- o paper
- ○ white thread
- o new moon water

Write the memory down on paper.

Roll the paper up with rosemary inside. Wrap entirely with white thread.

Submerge the package, then bury.

"Sweet Tooth" Spell Sachet

A simple sachet spell for renewal of innocence.

Gather rink rose buds and baby teeth, bless the bag with sugar mixed in full moon water.

Bleeding Candle Spell

A candle spell meant to cauterize an emotional wound.

Gather:

- preferred healing crystals
- rose petals
- rock salt
- rosemary
- a red and white candle each

Form a circle with the rock salt.

Arrange rose petals and crystals around the edge.

Place the white candle in the center.

Light the red candle and drip wax onto the white candle.

Speak aloud of the ways you are moving on and healing, or plan to.

Place a pinch of rosemary into the white candle's wick.

Light the white candle with the red, and burn the rosemary.

Blow out candles when you feel ready.

Flower Healing Spell

———————

A spell to heal with the influence of the sun.

Gather:

- a lily
- sun water
- gold glitter
- white and purple thread
- vanilla

Sprinkle the inside of the lily with the glitter and vanilla.

Close and wrap the lily up with the white and purple thread.

Lay the lily in the sun water, and sing/chant.

Drink the sun water. Take precaution not to consume glitter.

Brush you hair, comb it with the remaining sun water.

Rejuvenation Spell

A spell to for emotional healing from a particularly bad place to lift you up to a new place.

Gather:

- o fern
- o a white candle
- o quartz
- o object to represent your despair

Arrange the pieces of your despair on the ground.

Wrap the candle with the fern.

Light the candle, hold it up over the despair.

In your other hand, hold the quartz up to the flame, reflecting the light.

Wait until you feel the quartz is fully charged.

Extinguish the candle, and keep the quartz among the pieces.

Fire Element Bath

A bath spell that uses the element and correspondences of fire to heal and cleanse oneself emotionally.

Gather:

- anise
- cinnamon
- oranges
- red roses

Fill the tub with hot water, be careful not to make it too hot for you.

Mix ingredients into the tub. Light candles around the tub if you can.

Allow the element of water to cleanse your old energies out and the elements of fire to give you new energy.

Allow the heat to comfort and heal for as long as you need to.

Fire is associated with candles and blades. If you shave, this is a recommended time for it.

Though you can use garnet and ruby stones in the ritual, do not put them in the water, the aluminum in them is harmful when in water. Keep them nearby if you like.

Bleeding Heart Tea Potion

A tea potion made to soothe an emotionally injured heart.

Gather:

- o 2 parts cran-raspberry juice
- o 2 parts orange juice
- o 1 part pineapple juice
- o a pinch of cinnamon
- o 2 tea bags

Mix the juices over the stove on high heat.

Stir in the cinnamon.

Heat water, steep tea bags 5-10 minutes.

Mix juice into tea.

Serve warm.

Chant *"cor aut mors,"* before drinking.

Rose Quartz Shielding Spell

A shielding spell that both protect you from nearby people's negativity, and dispels peoples' negativity to a state where they feel loved, safe, and non-combative.

Gather:

- o rose quartz
- o coffee beans
- o an acorn
- o thread/string

- – Rose quartz for love and good feelings, healing
- – Coffee beans for protection and banishing negativity
- – Acorn for happiness

Craft a charm you can have on your person out of the materials, fill the charm with intent.

Charge and cleanse the rose quartz before using, to increase effectiveness.

Moon Circlet Magic

A spell to protect against people making rude comments to you, and spreading their negativity.

Gather:

- o   a pink ribbon
- o   moonstone or selenite
- o   bay leaf

Use the ribbon to tie the crystal and bay leaf together.

Create a sort of wearable circlet or bracelet.

When you needs its protection from others, wear the item.

Jupiter Banishment

A spell to banish toxic and dangerous people.

Gather:

- sea salt
- storm water
- a bay leaf
- flint

Combine the sea salt in the storm water until it dissolves

Soak the bay leaf in the water, then wrap it around the flint

Place the object near the doorway of your home, or bury it by the front doorstep.

Chant:

" On behalf of Jupiter, I call upon the forces of thunder and lightning to banish this person! "

Pluto Ending Spell

A spell to shut down things that are bothering you.

Gather:

- o pen/paper
- o tanzanite
- o black salt
- o harbor water
- o something representative of what you want to end

Mix the black salt and water.

Draw the symbol of Pluto and invoke its influence.

Soak the symbol of Pluto and the representative object in the mixture.

Ask Pluto to call for the end of it.

Use the scene from sailor moon crystal if you need/want to.

Shake It Out Spell

A spell to banish any spirits or people that have been pestering you.

Preferably done at night, or early in the morning.

Gather:

- paper
- chamomile
- coffee grounds
- bay leaf

On a piece of paper, write down the names of those who are plaguing you, people or spirits.

Fold up the paper into a heart.

Bury the heart in the ground with chamomile and coffee grounds.

Look to a new dawn.

Snow Drop Protection Spell

A floral charm to protect you from magic meant to cause you harm of grief.

The Snowdrop, or milkflower, is a harbinger of spring, signifying renewal and life at its most new and vibrant. From this, its use in magic the snowdrop is considered sacred and is a symbol of purity. It can be used to negate baneful magic and ill intents.

"The snowdrop, in purest white arraie,

first rears her hedde on candlemas daie."

— An Early Calendar of English Flowers

Gather:

- o   a snowdrop flower
- o   clear quartz

If no snowdrops are available, make one from craft supplies and consecrate it with dew, or melted snow.

Charge the snowdrop with the clear quartz. Seal it with a kiss before using it, as in the book it was bought for a kiss.

Attach it to an article of clothing when you wish it to protect you.

Gender & Orientation Spells

Spectrum Glamour

A glamour to feel alive, grand and brave, but most of all, to feel confident and be present.

Gather:

- candles one each white, blue, grey, candle, gold
- ocean water
- metal
- lavender
- something you will attach the glamour to. (ie: lipstick, a ring, worry stone)

Arrange the paper by the white candle, water by the blue, metal by the gray, lavender by the black, and the object in the middle.

Hold each object before you place it before the corresponding candle, spend a few long moments understanding the object with as many senses as you can. Then light the candle. Repeat for each object.

Say your name three times before you blow each candle out. Use the names you know yourself best by. Each time you say your name, kiss your palms.

Let the gold candle burn down a while before you blow it out last.

Pass the enchanted object through the gold candle's smoke. Wear/hold/use it when you need this glamour again.

Gender-Orientation Validation Spell

A spell to help one feel valid in their identity concerning gender and orientation.

Gather:

- orange peel
- rose quartz
- thyme
- thread

Make sure the thread represents the gender/orientation you're validating. You can use multiple threads and colors.

Sprinkle thyme in the orange peel. Wrap the orange peel around the rose quartz.

Bind with the threads. Hold when you need that extra validation.

Hidden Secrets Spell

———————

A spell specifically to protect one's gender or orientation, to keep it safely hidden when you can't be out.

Gather:

- o a small box, a root from a garden (something nonpoisonous)
- o something that represents what needs to be hidden
- o rainwater

Clean the root with the rainwater. Dry as thoroughly as you can.

Put the object in the box, wrap the box up with the root.

Place the box in the left corner of a cupboard, closet, desk, etc. Keep it as far back as you can, under many things.

Take it out and open it when you don't need it anymore.

Curses

Return to Sender

_____

A spell which repels the curses, intents, and actions back to the sender.

Gather:

- o oil
- o storm water
- o jars
- o salt
- o a cloth sachet
- o cloves

Place cloves in the sachet, add bag to jar and fill partially with oil.

Let the cloves infuse with the oil overnight.

Dissolve the salt in the water.

Combine the clove oil and salt water in a jar, seal with wax.

Breezeblocks Curse

A curse to affect someone you resent for leaving you behind. They will feel a great difficulty/sluggishness when trying accomplishing what they left you to do.

Gather:

- o   honey
- o   cough syrup
- o   bathwater
- o   a scrap of their clothing

The concoction starts sweet, as things between you started.

Pour the honey in over the clothing scrap, followed by the cough syrup. Drown it in bathwater, contain it all in a jar.

Seal with a kiss and black wax, and hide it away.

Your Heart In My Hand Curse

A curse for those who've hurt you. When you squeeze the poppet heart they will be plagued by nightmares of what they did to you, and feel a general sense of being lost in life.

Gather:

- o a taglock
- o fabric to make the poppet heart, black or red.
- o a black candle
- o twigs, dirt, bugs

Light the candle. Take the taglock of theirs and make a poppet heart containing it. Fill it with dirt, twigs, and bugs (optional).

Construct and seal the poppet with black candle wax.

Bad Moon Rising Curse

A revenge based curse, designed to return the pain this person has inflicted on you from the new moon to the full moon.

Perform under a new moon.

Gather:

- a burnable object of theirs
- storm/hurricane water
- river water
- dirt from a foul place
- a black candle
- a bowl

Prepare the waters in advance by charging them under a full moon. Light the candle. Fill the bowl with the waters, let the empty night sky reflect in it. Mix the dirt in. Burn the object of theirs and mix the ashes in.

Bottle the mixture, store where the sun won't reach them. Sunlight touching the jar will undo the moon's influence.

Thorn In My Side Curse

———————

A curse for those that consistently abuse or hurt you. A spell to turn those that are a "thorn in your side" into a thorny consequence when they try to hurt you

Gather:

- o   red candle
- o   a thorn or something sharp
- o   a representative object of relationship
- o   something to represent the abuser

Light the candle and tilt it at an angle so the melted wax drips off the candle. Be very careful

Use the wax to encase the hair.

Prick yourself slightly with the thorn, or if the object has been used against you before, no need.

Press the thorn into the wax, and tell it,

> *"All that you have done to me, will be rebound onto you."*

Hide the ball of wax.

Burn Your Wishes Curse

A simple curse to keep someone's wishes from coming true.

Gather:

- seeded dandelions
- matches
- burn-safe area
- paper
- taglock

You can choose to make a ring of dandelions on the ground, or bundle, or simply use one. Note, the more dandelions the more wishes you destroy.

If you want to target specific wishes, write them down on slips of paper and wrap them around the stems of the dandelion

Place taglock in the middle of the circle, or around the bundle.

Burn the dandelions.

Dispose of safely. Keep the taglock.

Burst Your Bubble Curse

A simple curse to destroy someone's ego or their hopes over something.

Gather:

- a form of mist
- bubble juice or gum
- athame
- wine
- ash

Mix the ash and wine together clockwise. Speak of failure over them.

Carefully coat the sharp edge of the athame with the mixture.

Using smoke or vapour, whichever you prefer, fill a bubble.

For a sturdier bubble, you might use gum over bubble juice.

As you blow into it, visualize filling the bubble with their boasts.

Break the bubble with the sharp edge of the athame.

Curse for A Player

A curse from scorned lovers to the one breaking hearts, to give them difficulty finding anyone to be with romantically/sexually

Gather:

- something to represent the person you're cursing
- roses
- 1 rose bud
- matches
- fire safe surface
- black thread
- candle wax

Take the representative object and wrap it around the single rose bud

Burn the rest of the roses to ash. Roll the object in the ashes

Wrap with black thread, seal with wax. Keep in a jar.

'Red in Your Ledger' Curse

A curse to inflict all the pain a person has caused back on them, one item at a time.

Gather: a disposable notebook, red ink, matches, and a taglock.

Write down an itemized list of everything awful the person has done to you, and anyone else you know they have hurt. Fill the book if you must.

Bind it with the tag lock inside.

Chant three times:

"You must know you have debts to pay
And your scorned will collect one day."

Burn the book.

Curse of Warped Sight

———————

A curse that makes a person only see the most ugly aspects of themselves and others around them.

Gather:

- o a mirror
- o something to write on glass
- o a taglock
- o rose petals
- o a candle
- o a fire-safe surface
- o a cloth

On the mirror, draw an eye.

Add sigils for specific things you want the person to notice.

Place the taglock on top of the mirror.

Burn the rose petals to ash.

Scatter the cooled ash over the mirror's surface.

Cover with a cloth, do not look at the mirror after this.

To remove the spell, clean the mirror off without looking at it directly

Made in the USA
San Bernardino, CA
13 November 2018